AF115252

SLAYER

CHEYANNE BOOK SERIES | ONE

SLAYER

CHEYANNE ROSIER

Universal Write Publications LLC

Universal Write Publications LLC
237 Flatbush Avenue, Suite 107
Brooklyn, NY 11217
www.Universalwrite.net

Ordering Information:
Quantity sales. Special discounts are available on quantity purchases by corporations, associations, schools and others. For details, contact the publisher at the address above.
Orders by U.S. trade bookstores and wholesalers please contact Lightning Source.
Printed in the United States of America

For my parents.

1

Aera passed through the halls of the Great Tower, feeling her heart beat at an alarming speed. The tower had been built centuries before she was born, created upon the backs of the misfortunate. The structure was composed of silver and gold, an intricate composition that was still considered to be a fine work of art. Aera was not impressed by the tower. She couldn't be, knowing that the blood of millions had been spilled on the very ground on which she walked. Years ago, there had been a great battle to keep the tower standing. The northern countries lay siege against her place of birth, hoping to destroy their symbol of prosperity. Foolishly, civilians believed that if they camped out in front of the tower, armed with broomsticks and crosses, they would be able to ward the enemy away peacefully. Those civilians were wiped out without a second glance. From that day, the colors of her nation became gold and red. The gold was to represent the power of their people; the red to represent the blood that was spilled in order to protect them. Two gold and red swords were slung across her back, heavy in a way that was as familiar as the sound of her own voice. She knew the history all too well.

Shaking her head to clear it, she quickened her pace. Her bare feet slapped against the ground as she kept her eyes trained on the silver tile. Her mouth was set in a grim line. The Royal Guard had summoned her for a meeting, claiming that the issue was pressing, urgent. The last time they'd said such a thing, several homes were burnt to a crisp after a serial bombing; fifteen casualties. She neared two mahogany doors and threw them open, ignoring the lush tapestries and carefully formed sculptures. After glancing upwards momentarily, she trained her eyes on the ground. She fell to one knee, closing her eyes and holding her hand against her heart. It beat wildly beneath her fingers.

"I am here, my lords." Her voice echoed in the vast space. Several other voices echoed the same phrase, some light and feminine, others a deep masculine baritone.

A soft voice answered them, amusement laced in their tone. "Welcome, tainted ones. We are pleased that you were able to arrive in a timely manner. We call you forth with grave news."

Aera frowned. Something terrible must've happened for them to call upon her regiment. "What do you wish to speak with us about?" She asked, her gaze still fixed on the plush red carpet lining the floors.

A deep chuckle followed her question. "Rise, Commander."

Aera knew the voice well. A small smile grew on her face as she stood. The voice grew louder, as if the person had walked closer. She took a deep breath as warm air washed over her face.

"Our kingdom is being faced by a terrible danger, something only you can help us with." The man bent his head so he was in Aera's line of vision, and she immediately squeezed her eyes shut. He sighed and turned to the circle of lords and ladies, a deep frown on his handsome face. "Why must they do that?"

A cold voice answered, polite yet bitter. "Such is tradition. No person of violence may look upon the holy creatures that we are. They are tainted by the blood of enemy soldiers, outcasts. You can see it in their eyes."

Aera wished to contradict, but lowly as she was, she couldn't even dare to do such a thing. She lifted her eyes to the man, knowing exactly what he'd see. As a commander, her and her seven captains had been subjected to a painful transformation. All eight of them now had a pair of silver, swirling eyes that seemed to contain all the knowledge in the universe. It was a beautiful curse. "Lord Demetrix, she is correct. I am tainted; no Royalty should be exposed a person of such violent nature."

Lord Demetrix gasped and took a step back, his face the picture of confusion. His hair was shaggy and black, falling into gold eyes that lay under his furrowed brows. His face was angular and handsome, his body dressed in gold and red robes that reached the ground. Aera looked back down when he took another step back. He looked exactly the same as she'd remembered. "What happened to your eyes?" He hissed under his breath and turned on his companions. "What did you do to her?"

Lady Lylax answered before he could speak again. She sounded sad. "We changed their eye color. It is only to warn the citizens of how much bloodshed she has caused. All of them," she gestured, "are leaders of the Royal Elite. No matter how you look at it, they are dangerous. Such power cannot be released into the lives of the civilians."

Lord Demetrix sighed angrily, and lowered his voice to a whisper. "I'll find some time to talk to you soon. I promise."

Aera opened her eyes to watch his golden shoes as he walked away. She let out a breath she hadn't realized that she'd been holding, feeling her pulse race. Demetrix had been her childhood friend, but as their positions changed, so did their relationship. He was the leader of the kingdom, and she was his faithful servant. She hadn't seen his face in years.

She walked forward a few steps and cleared her throat. "What exactly is this danger?"

"Demons," a voice replied simply, as if it were a normal occurrence instead of a completely insane notion that couldn't possibly be anything but pure fiction. Aera felt her mouth drop open in alarm. Of all the things they could've possible said, this is what they call her for!

"I beg your pardon?" She tripped over her words, feeling slightly offended at the fact that they'd called her only to pull her leg. *They don't have anything better to do?* She thought to herself. She could imagine their faces, covered in wide grins as they struggled to contain their laughter.

"There have been several demon attacks." The voice belonged to Lord Ashfall, the leader of the Royal Guard. He sounded serious, and this worried Aera even more. "At first we thought there was a normal serial killer, but after we examined several bodies, it is clear that the murderer is anything but human." A squire rushed over to her, and she lifted her head slightly to gaze at him as he handed her a manila envelope. He was short and plump, with thinning brown hair that grew in patches along his shiny head. The squire had an air of confidence about him, as if he were the king, and not just a messenger. She peeled open the envelope and took out several photos of dead bodies. All of them were mangled, the bodies torn in pieces, bones scattered across the scene as the blood of the victims ran freely across the ground. She cringed and handed them back. The squire bowed at the waist and then scurried back to his leaders' sides.

"And how did you come to the conclusion that we could *beat* whatever is doing this?" Aera fought to keep her voice steady as the gruesome images flashed in her mind.

"It is because you are the Royal Elite. This is your duty." The person who answered sounded bored. "You are dismissed. We expect this to be done within a month. Are we clear?"

"Yes, my lords." Aera spoke between clenched teeth. She turned around and raised her eyes, storming out of the room and snapping for her captains to follow. They rose and met her with varying silver gazes. The captain of the first squadron, an eighteen year old boy by the name of Ethan, looked worried as he addressed his commander. "Demons don't exist...right Aera?"

"I haven't encountered one in my nineteen years of existence." She replied. "On the other hand, I wouldn't be too surprised, considering what I *have* encountered in my nineteen years of existence. But the Royal Guard claims that demons have been killing off people in the kingdom. Even if they aren't demons, we have to stop the murders."

The second squadron captain nodded in agreement. "This is true. And besides, I'm not afraid to get a little blood on my hands." He rubbed them together like he could feel the blood running through his fingers. He raised his eyes to meet Aera's and gave her his award winning smile. "And if worse comes to worse, we have Aera on our side. Nothing could possibly go wrong."

Aera appreciated the blind faith he had in her, and gave him a light smile. "Why thank you Marcus." She turned to the youngest captain, a sixteen year old girl named Scarlett who controlled the third squadron. Her hair was so black it seemed blue, and her hair flowed around her shoulders in waves. "What do you think about this?"

Scarlett pulled out a large syringe from her pocket and held it up. "I've always got this! If anything goes wrong, we'll just inject 'em with this and all our problems will be solved."

Aera felt her right eye twitch. *Who the hell keeps a thirteen inch needle in their pocket?* As if sensing her bewilderment, Scarlett said: "I walked here alone, so I brought this along in case one of the higher class children tried to jump me." She glanced at her feet, looking contrite. "Last time they got me, I injected them with the blue experiment liquid instead of the red one, and the kid ended up in a coma for three weeks." She held up the needle again, moving so suddenly that all the captains took a few steps back. "That's why this time, I brought the green one!"

Aiden, the fourth captain, brought his hand to his face, shaky his head with a lazy grin. "What are we to do with you Scarlett?"

The sixteen year old didn't even blink. "I believe you should use me for my vast knowledge of poisons and medicines in order to successfully complete any mission that we have been assigned."

Aera felt her eye twitch again as she peered closely at the young girl. *Something is seriously wrong with her.* Trying to lighten the mood, she clapped her hands together and looked around at her seven companions. "Let's go on patrol, shall we? We only have a month to get this thing done, anyway."

Lauren, the fifth squadron captain, looked hesitant. "Can we go to The House first? I'm starving." To add to her point, her stomach growled.

The commander sighed and looked around at her unit. "We'll get food on the way to the murder scene. We all know that if we go to The House, the guys are going to start playing video games, and we girls are going to try and swim in the pool. We'd never leave." The captains murmured reluctant agreements.

Aera smiled kindly at them. "Besides, according to the Guard, we're nothing but ruthless killers. We might as well be robots." Luke, the sixth captain, and Julie, the seventh, laughed in agreement. Scarlett made her body as stiff as a board, walking in a mechanical way as they headed out of the Great Tower. They all laughed at her demonstration, but as soon as they exited the building, they became stone-faced, emotionless. *After all, we have a reputation to maintain.* Aera thought. She led the unit, her eyes squinting against the harsh sunlight as she moved swiftly down the large granite stairs that lead to the Tower. Her captains followed closely behind her, not uttering a word. She let out a loud whistle when she reached the bottom of the stairs, causing the seven people behind her to stop. Ethan walked up to Aera's side, letting out a similar whistle. The other captains followed suit. Suddenly, the light was blocked out, the sun no longer visible in the sky. A few civilians shrieked in fear, but the Royal Elite wore matching smug smiles.

With a thundering sound, a large creature landed a few feet in front of them, it's wingspan a total of seventy five feet. Its body was silver and black, covered in intricate designs that swirled like glyphs on its skin. It let out a roar, the remaining sunlight glinting off of sharp teeth that were built for mauling. Folding its wings against its back, it took one large step and leaned towards Aera, who smiled at it and patted its bent head. The creature let out a purring sound, blinking wide silver eyes at her. "Hello Rebellion." She said softly. Several people stared in horror at the large reptile, and Lauren turned to them, her expression blank. "You all act like you've never seen a dragon before. We go through this every time the Guard summons us. Besides this little girl has something far scarier in her pocket." She pointed bluntly at Scarlett, who took it as her cue to pull the ridiculously large needle from her pocket. The crowd dispersed before she could say more, and Luke tapped the glass that held the green experiment liquid. "Huh, I guess this came in handy after all."

Aera shook her head at their antics and got on Rebellion, who rose two hundred feet with one swift down-beat. She looked up, where seven more dragons were circling overhead. They took a spiraling dive, each landing in front of their owners with a loud shriek. The captains patted their dragons before getting on and following Rebellion into the air. Rebellion let out an ear-splitting roar before soaring swiftly towards the horizon. Aera pulled out a small device that the Guard used to contact her. Lists of crime locations were printed on the screen, and she scrolled upwards to the first one. She leaned towards her dragon's ear, pushing away the large whisker-like things that protruded from his head. The whiskers flowed in the wind, helping the dragon sense danger. "Go to Catalai," she whispered.

Aera loved the feeling of the wind through her hair. The soft evening breeze brushed lightly across her face, scented like roses and sea-salt. She smiled, glancing back at her captains, who'd fallen fast asleep on their dragons' backs.

It wasn't long before Rebellion stopped, bringing the other dragons to a halt behind him. They hovered over a large castle that sparkled so much; it could've been made of diamonds. Rolling hills surrounded the castle, small houses dotting the grassy plains. Closer to the castle, however, a small city rippled out like waves, buildings high, and low and in between. A forest surrounded the entire area, growing in a wide, even circle. Suddenly, Rebellion dived, the unexpected rush of air causing Aera to gasp. When they landed, a loud, thunderous sound emitted, leaving the ground dented.

Aera shifted her two swords on her back, sliding down the dragon's outstretched wing until her feet touched the ground. Rebellion and the other dragons disappeared into the sky. Running her hands through her now messy hair, she turned to her other captains, who awaited instruction. She pointed to Luke and Lauren, her tone letting them know it was time to get down to business. "Alright, you two, go to the civilians. See if they know anything about these *demons.*" She turned to the rest of the captains. "Ethan, Marcus, and Aiden, you three check out the city. Make sure you scan the castle too." They nodded. "Julie, Scarlett, you two are with me. We're going to head out into that forest."

Once they'd divided into groups, Aera looked at Julie and Scarlett. Scarlett was the leader of the third squadron, which specialized in chemical warfare. The sixteen year old girl pulled another syringe out of her pocket; it was filled with a hazy yellow liquid. Aera narrowed her eyes. "What is that?"

"A chemical that I will place in this aerosol can to spray on a few trees...maybe a rabbit." She stated it matter-of-factly, as if it were obvious.

Aera narrowed her eyes even more. "What does it do?"

The girl looked up, staring at her with wide silver eyes. "I don't know."

Aera fought the urge to smack her head against a tree, and slowly brought the girl to her feet. "Alright, do what you must."

She placed the valve containing the yellow liquid inside of the can, then sauntered up to a tree and pressed the button. Thick yellow smoke erupted from the can, surrounding the tree and then disappearing into nothingness. They waited a few moments to see a reaction, but nothing happened. Scarlett looked disappointed. "I guess it doesn't do anything then." She turned to walk away, but was stopped by a quiet voice saying, "wait."

She turned quickly, only to see a young man standing where the tree once was. His skin was brown, like the tree trunk, and covered with a rough substance, like bark. His hair was long and forest green, flowing down to his waist. He had a very prominent jaw with high cheekbones, his eyebrows thick and arching. His eyes were the same hazy yellow as the chemical.

Julie was startled, staring wide-eyed at the tree boy. "Why did you create a liquid to turn things into humans? Why would we ever need that?"

Aera held up her hand and Julie was quiet. "Maybe he's seen something. After all, people aren't cautious about what they're saying when they're surrounded by trees."

The tree boy was curious, looking around with questioning eyes. He looked at Scarlett. "You turned me into a human." It was a statement more than a question, but Scarlett felt the need to answer anyway.

"Yes, I did. I am the brave woman who sprayed that questionable gas onto your plant body and turned you into a man. Is there a problem? If there is, I'm sure I can find some plants and create a mixture that would transform you back into a boring old tree. You could stand right there for the rest of your life, looking directly at the sun like you aren't supposed to."

Aera could've sworn she saw the boy's eyes flash in annoyance. She stifled a laugh and covered the young girl's mouth before she sent the kid running into the hills. "I am Aera, the leader of the

Royal Elite. We are here to search for some suspicious characters who have been murdering innocent people. As a tree, did you witness anything?"

The boy looked thoughtful as he considered it. "A few nights ago, three men passed through the woods, but they looked funny."

Aera felt her heart sink. "Funny in what way?"

The boy took a moment before responding. "They were hunched over, and they drooled all over my feet." He grimaced. "They kept saying things like 'curse' and 'death.' Plus, they must've been a whole lot heavier than they looked, because their footsteps rang out as if they were giants." He tilted his head to one side, like a dog. "Is that enough information for you?"

Aera nodded, letting go of Scarlett who demanded that she apologize before she got out the orange experiment fluid. She nodded shortly and turned to Julie. As the captain of the seventh squadron, her specialty was informational work. She pulled out a computer and typed a few words. Then Julie turned to the tree boy, who stood stiff, bending slightly with the wind as if he were still a tree. "When was this again?"

"July 12, 3034." He responded quietly, not opening his eyes to look at her.

Julie typed the date and her eyes widened in disbelief. "Aera... you might want to see this..." She trailed off, her eyes glued to the screen. Aera walked over and looked over the captain's shoulder, and immediately, she wanted to cover her eyes.

"What the—" Both Julie and Aera silenced Scarlett before she could get in another word. The first footage was of a man with black hair and stunning eyes that shone an icy blue. His skin was light, pale. There was another man with him, who was significantly shorter, with short cropped blond hair and dark red eyes. They were leaning against a tree, their lips pressed together.

"Whoa, are they kissing?" Scarlett asked.

Julie pushed Scarlett away without looking away from the screen. Aera looked closely at their faces, and she found herself recognizing one of them. "I-Isn't that...your brother, Scarlett?"

Now interested, Scarlett peered closely at the taller man. "Hey, I think you're right. I didn't know he was into guys." An evil look passed over her face. "I can't wait to see his face when I show him this video."

Aera ignored her and focused on the video. One of the hunched over people that 'tree-boy' described was walking steadily towards the couple. Black goo dripped from his parted lips, and his eyes were rolled into the back of his head. Scarlett frowned, but didn't say anything. Suddenly the hunched over man stopped, turned around, and headed in the opposite direction. His feet were sinking deep into the soil with each step he took.

"You are not marked for death..." The man said. "You are not cursed."

The man who Scarlett's brother was kissing opened his eyes for a spit second and made a strange gesture to the 'demon.'

Aera caught the gesture at record speed. "Find that man, Julie."

For a split second, Aera looked back at Scarlett, who'd set upon texting her brother. Creepy chuckles came from the girl's mouth as she grinned at the phone in her hands. It looked like she'd ignored everything in the video besides the fact that Matthew, her brother, was kissing another guy. The girl was hopeless. Deciding to put the girl's issues on the backburner, she turned to Julie, who was hard at work on her computer.

"I clipped the photo of the man and I'm searching him now." When the results popped up, she looked confused. "My archive says that the information is blocked."

"What?" Aera looked at the computer where the words 'Access Denied' were flashing across her screen. "That's strange." Aera tried typing a few codes in, but still, those words were flashing across the screen. Suddenly, the words shifted into small red characters.

"What does that say?" Aera asked quietly.

"I don't know," Julie responded. "It is written in an ancient language. A language that uses characters instead of words."

Aera closed her eyes and remembered each character, watching the words form behind her lids. Before she knew it, she was reading out loud. "To find the one you seek, listen closely. There are two people, their hearts repel each other. They know the man, the one you're searching for, yet each one knows only part of the information that you need. Find them both, bring them to each other. Find the opposites and bind them."

Julie fixed Aera with a blank stare. "What?"

Aera pulled out a pen and a paper, writing the words down. "Okay, so there are two people we need to find. Apparently they hate each other, but we need to bring them together. And...the opposites?" She furrowed her brow in confusion. "This makes no sense."

Scarlett looked at them, putting her phone in her back pocket. "Yes it does."

Tree Boy came up behind her and nodded in agreement. "The Prophesy of the Opposites. It's very old. Apparently, the world is reborn each time that all the Opposites are gathered in a special place. It is very hard to get them to that place, however, because they all hate each other so much. If memory serves, there is a crystal cavern that supplies them with enough energy to do the reset, but they only have the power to reset every few centuries. Frequent resetting drains their magic, and they can die."

Julie turned her blank gaze on him. "What?"

Tree Boy shook his head. "You see, there was a time where the world was dying off, and the people were in a panic. All the natural resources were gone, and each person was fighting to survive. People were dying left and right. Apparently though, our ancestors created a way for humans to reset the world, a fresh new start when there was nothing left. They made it difficult to do so the world wouldn't be reset on accident."

Aera looked at him. "And what do you mean by 'reset'?"

"Well..." he trailed off, "I think it depends on what you want them to do. In caveman days, they wanted to be free of their only natural predator, the dinosaur. They reset the earth, and bam!" He claps, making them jump. "Free men!"

"Does this mean that we have to reset the world?" Scarlett asked.

Tree Boy nodded grimly. "It must mean that. I've seen things like this many times." He held his head in his hands. "I'm a lot older than I look."

Scarlett couldn't help herself. "How old?"

Tree Boy looked at her and smiled. "Well, since I'm a giant sequoia and I never got cut down, I'd say about four thousand."

Julie turned her eyes back to her computer. "Well, you look like you're twelve."

Tree Boy sighed. "So, why do you think that you need to reset the world?"

"The demons are coming." A deep voice answered. They all turned around to see a tall man with small, cat-like hazel eyes. His hair was shaggy and black, falling into his face. He was dressed in all black, from his vest to his large combat boots. On his back, he strapped a large silver bow and a quiver filled with arrows. The arrows had three spiked heads, looking like launch able tridents. Hooked on one side of his black metal-laced belt, a whip was coiled like a snake. It had small knives protruding from each side, all of them stained crimson with blood. At the end of the whip was a black handle with a small red button at the bottom. On the other side of his belt were various, odd-shaped daggers.

Aera was immediately wary of him. "And you must be...?"

His face was completely emotionless. "The demons are coming."

"We understand that, could you tell us your name?" Julie spoke slowly, as if she were speaking to a small child. Still, they received no reaction.

"The demons are coming."

"While that is very nice, we'd love to know your name."

"The demons are coming."

"Why do you have so many weapons?" Scarlett tried.

"The demons are coming." This time, he reached for the whip, which unfolded at his side. His mouth twisted into a sick grin.

"Um..." Julie looked at Aera, who was looking closely at the boy.

"The demons..." the boy snapped the whip, causing the air around him to sizzle. He flashed them a smile, and then pressed the button at the bottom of the whip. The buzz of electric current was unmistakable. "The demons are here."

2

Luke looked quizzically at Lauren, who was hugging a small child to her chest. "Can we keep it?" She asked. A brilliant smile was on her face. The child gripped onto her arms, not seeming to mind being carried around like a doll. Luke felt his face fall.

"And what if, let's say, a demon attacks us. Do you think you can use your scythe with a small child in your hands?" Luke raised an eyebrow at her, expecting a rational response. Instead Lauren snatched her scythe off of her back and pressed the blade at his neck. The child in her hands clapped happily. "Go Lauren!" She giggled.

Luke pinched the bridge of his nose, pushing the scythe away.

"Okay, you've proved your point. But could you *please* give that back to its owner so we can move on to the next house? Aera would kill us if she knew that we've been sitting here for three hours hugging a two year old."

Lauren frowned. "Her name is Boo."

"Yes, yes, whatever." Luke waved off the correction. "Just give the baby back to its mommy so we can be on our way. We haven't interviewed even one family yet."

Lauren turned her attention back to the giggling baby, and ignored Luke.

He sighed and walked away, approaching a small, square home that looked like it was falling apart. Luke grew up in a home like that. In a way, the broken shutters and cracked, stained walls were familiar. He raised his hand to knock on the door, but before he did, it opened. A tall man stood there, with soft black hair and midnight blue eyes. There were bags under his eyes, and he'd wrapped a large wool blanket around his body. Looking tired, he asked, "Did Scarlett send you here?"

Luke took a step back. "Er...no. Why?"

"Don't lie to me!" The guy sounded furious. "I know you saw the video of me kissing him, alright? You don't have to lie about it." He sighed.

Luke took another step back. "Who are you again?"

"I'm Matthew Arctic."

"And I know you....how?"

"I'm Scarlett's brother."

Luke was gone before Matthew could get in another word. He rushed up to Lauren, breathing heavily as he heard Scarlett's brother calling after him. "We need to go, like, now." He pointed to the baby. "Grab that, and let's leave."

Lauren stood up. "Why?"

He pointed to Matthew, who was running steadily towards them. "That guy is related to Scarlett."

Lauren looked bored. "So?"

"That means he's probably crazy! There's a crazy person running towards you and your pet Boo, and you aren't going to run?" Luke exclaimed, beginning to sweat nervously as Matthew got closer.

"Good point. Let's go." She grabbed Boo and her teleporter, transferring them to a house far away, leaving poor Knight standing there, confused.

3

"Is this normal?" Aiden asked, staring at the craziness that was happening.

A silver whip streaked across the pale morning sky, meeting its mark with a sickening crack. The boy tied to the stake didn't flinch against the lash; instead he let out an inhuman roar that ended in a scream of agony. Blood poured out of the multiple gashes on his back, pooling onto the dusty ground beneath him. His hands trembled and the tips of his shaggy white hair had been dyed crimson. It was a gruesome scene. An older woman who appeared to be the boy's mother was standing at the front of the large crowd that had gathered. Her face was contorted with grief and tears ran down her face.

Ethan shoved his hands in his pockets, the picture of perfection, as always. His caramel colored skin shone in the sun like warm honey, his long brown hair pulled into a pony tail. He wore the typical lower-class clothing: torn jeans and a plain grey t-shirt that made his silver eyes seem darker. "Who knows what they do in Catalai. Everyone knows that the people here are strange." He nodded to the boy getting whipped. "But, I have to admit that that's a little much."

Marcus came back from a food stand with bags of cotton candy, but when he spotted the main attraction of the city, he stopped. "What are they doing to that kid?" He exclaimed, causing several people to turn around.

"He is being purged." A quiet voice answered. A girl no older that fifteen stood behind them, wrapped in middle-class robes. Her hair was short and white, like the boy's. She didn't look at them as she spoke.

"What is that?" Marcus asked quizzically.

"My brother has been sinful. The Keeper is helping to purge him of his sins so he doesn't become a demon. The Royal Guard demands that this should be done." Her voice was low, and when she glanced up, her eyes were silver. She seemed shocked at the fact that their eyes were the same color, and she took a step back. "You are marked. You have been marked for death, like me."

Ethan turned around. "What's taking you so long, Marcus? I'm hungry." When he saw the fearful expression on his friend's face, he looked around him to the girl, who looked even more appalled when she saw Ethan and Aiden's eyes.

"If you stay here, you all will die," her voice was quivering with fear. "You will die, just as my brother and I will: at the hands of a demon."

4

Aera whirled around to see that what once was an empty clearing was now full of hunched over men drooling goo.

"Look at their silver eyes..." they whispered. "They have been marked for *death.*"

Scarlett pulled two oddly shaped guns from their holsters, aiming at the swarm of demons. "Well Mr. Creepy, I personally think you could've given us a bit more warning."

Aera and Julie gave her a drone look, but she dutifully ignored it. The strange man ran head-first into the crowd, somehow wielding his whip in one hand and a dagger in the other with ease. Three demons jumped at him, and he soared into the air, jumping over them and slashing with both hands.

Nothing was left but a giant pile of blood and gore.

Scarlett put her guns back while her two friends stared in amazement. "I guess he didn't need our help after all." She pulled out a jar of purple fluid. "Shall I drug him?"

"No!" Aera and Julie exclaimed in unison, not taking their eyes off of the boy who'd begun to clean his weapons.

"Who...are you?" Aera approached him cautiously.

He glanced at her momentarily, and then resumed cleaning his blade. "I have no name. The few people I know, however, call me Slayer...my enemies call me The Nightmare."

"Slayer?" Scarlett sounded skeptical. "What kind of name is that?"

Julie elbowed her in the side, taking another look at Slayer. His black hair was shaggy, framing his face that was ruggedly handsome. He had a shadow of a beard on his face. Julie skipped over to Aera, a mischievous look on her pretty face. "Hey, he's kind of cute. I think we should add him to one of the squadrons...preferably mine."

Aera rolled her eyes at the captain and faced the young man sitting on the grass. "Is there anyone that you hate?" She asked, hoping that his mysterious appearance had something to do with The Prophesy.

"That's none of your business." He snapped. "I hate demons. That's all you need to know."

Scarlett looked down for a second, scratching her head. "Do you know anyone named like, The Daydream?" She gave a little laugh, but Slayer stiffened; his expression unreadable.

"I'd best be on my way." He slung the dangerous looking whip over his shoulder. "There are demons crawling everywhere." He looked down. "But...what's this I heard about resetting the world?" He turned around, and for the first time, Aera looked at his eyes. They were gold...like Demetrix's and the other members of the Royal Guard. What did that mean?

"Apparently we need to reset the world, but we don't know why."

He narrowed his eyes at her. Taking slow, lazy steps, he walked over to her. "And what makes you think the opposites will comply?"

It was her turn to narrow her eyes at him. "How did you know about the opposites?"

He gave her an impatient smile, tipping his head to the side and tightening his grip on the handle of his whip. "Let's just say that I'm a little special."

Without looking away, Aera pulled a device out of her pocket, bringing up the picture of the man Matthew was kissing. "Do you recognize this man?"

Slayer let a grin grow on his face. "And if I do?"

Aera was taken aback by the look on his face. He looked like he was about to burst out laughing. He pressed his lips together to stop from smiling.

"What in the world is so funny?"

He shrugged. "Well…it's just that…the guy in the photo and I have a strange past. It's an inside joke." He dismissed her, as if she couldn't possibly understand. "Anyway, that man owns a large restaurant in the city. You should be able to find him at this address." He pulled a piece of paper and a pen from his pocket and wrote the information down. "Is that all?"

Aera nodded. "Thank you, we appreciate it."

Slayer turned away. "I hope you find what you're looking for. But be careful. There are many things here that are set in stone, and anyone who messes with them faces dire consequences." In a flash of silver, two wings appeared on his back. He turned to face them momentarily. "Good luck." With that he soared into the sky, disappearing into the clouds.

Tree boy peered out from under a rock, his hands shielding his head. "Is it safe to come out yet?"

Aera opened her mouth to respond, but then everything went dark.

5

Slayer beat his wings hard against the wind, feeling the familiar sensations that came with flying. His thoughts were in a knot, and his heart beat faster when he thought of what the girl said. *They're going to try and reset the world again. It's only been a few centuries since the last reset.* He cursed under his breath. "Why can't these humans get it right for once?"

He dived sharply, plummeting towards the earth faster than light. When he reached the ground, he curved his wings, the delicate silver feathers acting as a parachute. His feet rested lightly on the grass, and he looked up at the large volcano that stood in front of him. There was a cave at the base of it, and he approached it wearily. The dark mouth stood hungrily above him. There was not a sound. As soon as he took a step forward, he felt a knife being held to his throat, strong hands pinning his arms behind his back.

"What business do you have here, Slayer?" A light, lilted voice asked.

"I'm just here to see The Protector." He sneered. "Or is that a problem, *Daydream?*"

The fingers around his wrists tightened, the nails digging into his skin. "You know I don't go by that name anymore *Nightmare.* I remember asking you politely to call me Myst." The girl released him and stood in front of the cave.

"Oh really?" Slayer scoffed. "I remember you shoving me into a wall and pressing a gun to my head *demanding* that I call you Myst."

"Whatever." She said. "What do you need the Protector for?"

He frowned. "Apparently the humans are planning on resetting the world again. I need to warn him."

She crossed her arms. "They're trying to reset the world again? Why in the world would they do that?"

"The demons have returned." He said, watching the way she stiffened.

"Then that is their fault. If the demons have returned, there is only one person who could summon them." Her eyes were fixed on an unknown point behind Slayer. "Lord Ashfall is the cause of this madness." Myst stepped aside. "Enter at your own risk."

Slayer passed through the murky depths of the cave. There was a winding dirt path lit by several torches on the walls. He sighed and shoved his hands in his pockets. There was a person standing up ahead. He recognized her immediately. "Hello Earth." He called her by her opposite name.

"Nightmare," she breathed. "It's been quite a while. You look well."

Slayer pulled her into a hug. "Don't act so polite. It makes me feel like a stranger."

"You are a stranger," she laughed. "I haven't seen you in decades. Have you seen that loner Sky lately? The Protector is searching all over for him."

He nodded. "Yeah, I ran into a couple humans on my way here, and they were kind enough to show me a picture of Ice's brother making out with him." He smiled.

"Whoa, that's interesting." She grinned.

Slayer shrugged. "Anyway, is the Protector in?"

She nodded enthusiastically. "Right this way."

They took a sharp right and entered a large chamber. It was significantly hotter in there, and beads of sweat formed along Slayer's forehead. Earth seemed unaffected. "The Protector is in there."

Slayer rested a hand on her shoulder. "Tell Daydream, 'no hard feelings,' ok?"

Earth barked out a sharp laugh. "She hates you, you know?" She turned sympathetic brown eyes on him. "It's only our nature to hate our opposite."

Slayer scratched his head. He smiled weakly. "What ever happened to opposites attract?"

Earth tilted her head to one side. "What happened to you two?"

Slayer's face turned hard, expressionless. "She started hating me when I killed a specific demon, which'd gotten turned by Ashfall. It turned out he was her boyfriend. Apparently girls don't like it when you kill their demon boyfriends. She said to me 'you really are a nightmare.' It hurt more than I expected it to." He sighed, feeling his shoulders sag. "It really doesn't matter." He turned around and headed into a separate room, even warmer than the last. There was a blazing fireplace in the corner, and several wooden bookshelves lining the rock walls. The large Oakwood desk on the farthest wall, and seated in a chair behind it was the Protector. He was less than human, considering that his long hair was made of fire, floating around his face. His eyes looked like rich coals, a deep, eerie orange glow coming from deep inside of them. Four of his teeth ended in sharp points, and his nails looked more like claws than anything else. He rose from his chair, and next to him were his two pet wolves stood, their teeth bared. Their fur was also made of fire, their eyes also black pits filled with orange flame. They opened their mouths, and let out deep growls. Suddenly, they began to speak.

"The Protector resides in a canyon of flame, he destroys any being who should curse his name, his eyes are rich coals, his hair is of light, and he protects all of Catalai with his strength and his might." They then bowed and disappeared into nothingness.

"I don't know why they feel the need to say that every time someone visits me." The Protector waved his hand and a large chair appeared next to Slayer. "Please sit."

Slayer sat down, knowing better then to reject an offer from the king of the opposites.

The Protector pulled a mug of steaming coffee from seemingly nowhere, taking a deep swig before turning back to Slayer. "What brings you here, Slayer?"

"Well, on my way here, I ran into a group of humans. They said they received some message saying that they need to reset the world again. Apparently the demon population is rising faster than expected. I can't control it."

The Protector pinched the bridge of his nose. "And the humans think that they can reset the world to get rid of the demons?" He laughed, "Ashfall is the source of all our problems, isn't he?"

Slayer cracked his knuckles. "You want me to get rid of him?"

The Protector smiled. "I wish it were that easy. He's just slightly immortal." The Protector walked over to Slayer. "He must be up to something though." He shook his head. "He's never turned this many people into demons since medieval times."

Slayer stood quickly. "Well, I think Sky has something to do with it."

"What?" The Protector frowned. "There's no way. I know that your friend Earth hates him, but that doesn't mean that you should say something bad like that about him."

"No," Slayer shook his head. "The humans I met showed me a picture of him gesturing to a demon. He told it not to attack." Slayer decided not to tell him about how he sent the humans after Sky as payback.

"Also, I saw Ice with the humans. She didn't blow my cover though." Slayer felt his brows furrow. "Maybe she's up to something too."

The Protector seemed to consider this. "Go find her. Find Ice and the humans, and watch how she interacts with Sky."

Slayer nodded and exited the room, turning back to the Protector. "What should I do if they're traitors?"

The Protector's eyes grew fiery. "Just bring them to me and I'll deal with it."

Slayer nodded. On his way out of the volcano, his mind wandered back to Daydream. He hadn't meant to kill her boyfriend. He was just doing his job as the Demon Slayer. He scoffed. *Why did she cheat on him with a demon anyway?* He spat on the ground, pushing his damp hair from his eyes. *I say good riddance.*

6

Ethan looked up at the castle, impressed by the elaborate crystal structure. "I wonder how long it took them to build this." He looked towards Aiden and Marcus, who were heatedly engaged in an argument about the Catalai government.

"Last time we visited Catalai, we went through this." Aiden said, his voice shaking with anger. "We agreed that the Jurenthian Government was better."

"I remember nothing of the sort." Marcus crossed his arms. "Even though I'm perfect, and smart, and handsome, and—for Guard's sake pay attention Aiden. Even though I'm all of those things, I have a bad memory."

Ethan sighed. "Aera said to look at this castle, so that's what we need to do." He pulled a flyer out of his pocket. "It says here that the castle was built in 2130." He sucked in a breath through his teeth. "Wow, this thing is pretty old." He turned to see that his friends still weren't paying attention. Raising his voice, he looked behind the quarreling pair. "Oh hello Aera. I was trying to get them to inspect the castle with me, but they said 'politics are more important.' Is it time for punishment?"

At these words, Aiden and Marcus jumped to their feet, trying to come up with decent apologies. They looked at the floor. "We're sorry Commander!" Aiden sighed.

"Yes...but just so we are clear, this was all Aiden's fault." Marcus said.

When they looked up, however, a guy with short blond hair and big red eyes was standing there. "You tricked us!" The two captains exclaimed, turning to Ethan with murderous intent. Ethan's eyes were trained on the guy behind them.

"Who are you?" He asked.

The blond man chuckled. "My name is James Sky. I own that restaurant."

Ethan glanced around, his arms crossed over his chest. "What restaurant?"

James pointed to the castle behind him. "The restaurant is right there. It's called Crystal Palace."

"No way," Ethan drawled sarcastically.

"Well, if you'd like to come in, I'd be happy to have you." James began to walk towards the castle.

Aiden pointed to the castle, his eyes wide. "No way that is a restaurant."

Marcus snickered. "Didn't you hear the man who *owns* the place? He said it's a restaurant."

Aiden narrowed his eyes at Marcus. "Well excuse me for being shocked by its extravagance."

Ethan sighed again. *It is going to be a long day.*

7

Lauren re-appeared with Luke inside of a river. Luke cursed at her, while she covered the baby's ears.

"@@#@%^$^%$%^#$%!" He said. "$^$&^@$%%&@# $!$@#$%^%^#$!"

Lauren gasped, covering her mouth with her free hand. "How rude. And in front of Boo, this poor, innocent little baby."

Luke snatched Boo from her arms and stomped out of the water.

"Hey, give that back!" Lauren hissed.

"Never!" Luke took off, heading towards a house. *Maybe this way we can get some work done."*

Suddenly, he heard Lauren scream. When he turned around,

she wasn't there. He opened his mouth to call for her, but was cut off when something hard knocked against his head. The last words he heard were: "Come here Boo."

8

Aera groaned, rolling over onto her back. She couldn't remember anything but waking up there. Painful wounds stung on her body, and she sat up, feeling thick linen beneath her body. She pulled the rough wool blanket tighter around her body, ignoring the painful friction that it caused against her skin. The concrete beneath her was cold, adding to the frigid morning air that bit at her body. She looked around, surprised to find herself in a box-like room full of thirty or so people. Some of them appeared to be no older than five, while others could easily be twenty. The walls were made of grey stone, unadorned and covered with rust colored stains that reached down like arms. There was a tiny space that'd been raggedly cut high on one wall. The open slot was full of metal bars that were jabbed in the flagstone at seemingly random angles. Dim light filtered through the make-shift window, illuminating the dull floor. There was a large brass door with several large locks on it, and Aera knew immediately that there was no way out of the cell. There was a pungent smell filling the room, a mixture of stale urine and death. She stood up, her bare feet leaving bloody stains on the ground. The coarse wool blanket fell around her ankles, landing with an almost inaudible thump. Several heads raised and turned her way. The chatter of their teeth was a quiet chorus, accentuating the sound the heavy breathing of those who were still asleep.

One girl, her hands and feet bound by thick copper chains, pinned Aera with dark silver eyes, a crimson liquid covering her mouth. Long claws formed at the ends of her fingers, and when she smiled at Aera, her teeth were set with sharp tips. Aera couldn't help but grimace in response. Panic began to build in her throat, but it was quickly replaced with a burning curiosity. *Where am I?* The sound of metal dragging on the floor made her turn, where a young boy was walking slowly towards her. He was at least five inches taller than Aera, and his hair was as white as snow. His eyes were a dull, stormy color. He grinned at her with the same pointy canines, that'd been dyed red with what she could easily assume was blood. He stopped a few centimeters away from her. He bent down to her; his face inches from Aera's, and inhaled deeply.

Her eyes were wide; she couldn't move, couldn't speak. When he moved away, Aera let out a breath that she hadn't realized that she'd had been holding. He pinned her with his cold, calculating silver gaze, not looking away for what seemed like hours.

"You smell like one of us, but you don't look like one of us." He cocked his head to one side, much like a dog would. "Can you tell me why that is?"

Aera opened my mouth to speak, but she had no answer. She felt chilly breath on her neck, and nearly leapt out of her skin when she realized that another one of the children—a girl—was taking deep breaths with her nose pressed against her neck. Aera gasped and jumped away. This girl's eyes were as dark as coals, her skin lacking color.

"She is one of us." The girl hissed. "Look at her eyes." She gestured to Aera's face, her claws millimeters from scratching her eyes out. She grabbed Aera's hand, and pulled it up to her eye level. Her nails were far shorter than the other children's, but they were still an animalistic length.

The silver-eyed boy growled deep in his throat, a mad look in his eyes. "But look at her teeth. If she is like us, why does she have human teeth?"

The girl seemed a bit thrown off, and roughly grabbed Aera's face, jabbing her grimy fingers into the Commander's mouth.

She tried to scream, and pressed her hands into the girl's chest, shoving hard. She flew into the opposite wall, leaving a dent in the rock. She slumped against the wall, a trickle of blood dripping from her parted lips. Aera covered her mouth, her eyes wide with shock as she stared at the girl's body, unmoving, several feet from where she stood. She stared at her hands, observing everything from her caramel toned skin to the black mud caked under her nails. *What am I?*

The silver-haired boy smiled at Aera, and she stepped back in alarm. *Why is he smiling? I just killed someone!* He pointed at the dead girl in the corner, and then pointed to himself.

"I've been trying to kill that disgusting vagrant since the moment I met her. You did it on your first try. Good job, newbie." He walked to the dead body and spat bitterly on the girl's bare feet. "Good riddance, I'd say."

Aera's mouth felt dry, but she managed to croak out a few simple words. "Where are we?"

The boy grimaced. "We're on our way to the Camps. We've been sentenced to life as outcasts." He sighed, sitting down next to where Aera stood tense, not daring to move an inch.

"Why?"

He barked out a harsh laugh, causing some of the other children to stir in their sleep. "It's because we're demons, of course. Humans capture every one of us that they discover."

Aera was confused. *But I am human, aren't I?*

He looked up at her, his lips set into a hard line. "Where are my manners?" He stuck out a mud covered hand, and she shook it loosely. "I don't know what my name was before they swiped my memory, but everyone here calls me Phantom."

She gave a weak smile and sat beside him. "I don't remember my name either."

Phantom laid his head back on the wall, and looked towards the large metal door. "Let's call you Spirit. You seem like a wayward spirit." He smiled kindly at Aera.

She nodded tiredly and looked away, her eyes drifting shut.

Her eyes snapped open at the sound of the large locks being opened. Aera shot to her feet as the children around her began to get up almost mechanically. They formed into a line, not even pausing as they walked over the dead girl's body. Looking around, she saw that there were many other still bodies lying on the pavement. Aera's blood went cold. Phantom gave her a small push and she walked stiffly into the line. *How can I get out of here?* The brass door began to move slowly open, letting out groans occasionally as if it was too heavy for the momentum to move it. Aera wasn't sure what she was expecting—maybe a buff man with short shorts and an eight pack—but a short woman stood on the other side of the door, flanked by two burly men. Her brown hair was cropped short, her eyes emotionless as she stared at the line. She took one step into the room, and wrinkled her nose at the smell. Her eyes filled with hatred as her gaze moved down the line.

When her eyes rested on Aera's, her mouth curled into a sneer. "Welcome to Purgatory, demons. By the time I'm done with you,

you trifling creatures will wish that you'd never been born. Every group of thirty-six demons at this camp are assigned a Keeper. I am yours. You will address me as Keeper Nancy or just Keeper. If I hear anything other than that," she paused, "well, let's just say you won't enjoy what happens to you. Now, you guys aren't just here to rot for the rest of your days. You'll be working to help the citizens of Jurenthis, the country located several thousand miles from where you stand. You will all be divided in three groups."

She pointed to the demons towards the front of the line. "You creatures will mine coal." She gestured towards the middle of the line. "You will create all the products that the citizens of Jurenthis will be using." She moved down to where Phantom and 'Spirit' stood. "The demons at the back will make the food and clean the compound." She passed a lingering glare at Aera, and then exited stepped back into the foyer. "To my left is a bathroom. Clean yourselves and then get to work." She snapped at her bodyguards and then disappeared into the hallway. Slowly, and in single file, the demons shuffled towards the bathroom.

Aera let out a hiss of pain when she entered the large room, noticing that large pieces of broken glass had been scattered over the cracked yellow tile. Some places were red with blood, and the shower stalls were covered with black mold and mildew. There was another barred window towards the end of the room. She glanced back at Phantom, who'd taken off his shirt and stepped into the stall, closing the torn curtain. Aera stepped into her own stall, coughing at the dusty smell. After she closed the curtain, she peeled the dirty, bloody clothing from her body. Shockingly, there were several large gashes on her back and arms. Now that she'd seen them, pain buzzed throughout her body. She shivered and turned on the water.

The clear liquid was scalding hot, burning her wounds. She cried out in pain and jumped out of the stream. She heard screams around her as well. Aera looked up, where a tiny camera and speaker were wedged in the corner of the stall. A crackling sound emitted from the speaker before a voice began to speak.

"Hello Spirit," It sneered. "Welcome to your own personal hell. If I were you, I'd do my best to hide my fears. If those disgusting creatures around you don't use them against you I will." A static laugh made the transmission sound harsh, and she stared up at the camera in horror. They turned the heat up on purpose because of her wounds!

She stepped into the stream again, and this time, she began to wash myself with the boiling water. Her skin wasn't bubbling, so she figured that because she was a demon, she could feel pain, but she couldn't be wounded easily. *I must've gone through something awful to retain the wounds on my body.* She was almost glad that they erased her memory of that. Dirty, bloody ran down her body in rivulets and circled around before going down the drain. Steam rose around her. Aera held in the screams that bubbled in her throat, and once she felt that she'd proven her point, she turned off the water and dried herself off. Aera wrapped a ripped up towel around her body in an attempt to cover up, and stepped outside. All the other demons had gathered around one corner of the room, and naturally, she went over to see what was there. Several shelves were on the walls, each one labeled with a name. The shelves had clothes, and some sort of identification engraved on dog tags. Aera looked for the shelf labeled 'Spirit' and grabbed her clothing. She assumed that they knew her new name because of the cameras everywhere. Now that she knew that they were there, there seemed to be one in every corner.

There were loose fitting sweatpants, underwear and a white shirt that had suspicious red stains on it. Aera shuddered and slipped the clothes on. Everyone else had disappeared into the stalls. She looked at the silver dog tag as she slipped it around her neck. It said:

Wayward, Spirit, Class A Demon, Female, Squadron 3, Owned by: Keeper Nancy.

The words rang in her head, and she dropped the tag as if it'd burned her. Owned. Phantom came up behind her and tapped her shoulder. Aera jumped, and he smiled knowingly, showing her his tag.

Phantom, Image, Class A Demon, Male, Squadron 3, Owned by: Keeper Nancy.

Aera felt tears pricking at her eyes as Phantom stared down at the tag in her hand. "So, are we emotionless beings who don't care what is said about them? Are we useless because we aren't human?" She demanded. "Are we nothing because we're demons?"

To Aera's surprise, Phantom pulled her into a hug, and put his mouth close to her ear. "We're breaking out of here. I've already made an arrangement." He smiled tightly. "He'll be here for us soon. We just need to lay low for a while."

A glimmer of hope filled the old Commander, and Phantom steered her out of the room, gently tugging on her arm.

Outside of the cell was no better than inside.

Dozens of demons were chained together, hauling heavy boxes of steel towards a large truck. The air smelled of smoke and iron, small concrete houses littering a vast amount of land. The camp went for as far as the eye could see. Older male demons were hauling lumber, their muscles bulging under the strain. A body was being burned near a tent. Several humans—Aera could tell by their cleanliness and aura of authority—stood by with silver, gold, and bronze whips coiled at their waists like snakes.

"I guess those are the other Keepers." She murmured quietly.

There was a bronze whip. There was a demon boy tied to a metal pole in the center of the camp. There were about ten deep, bloody gashes on his back. He looked older, around twenty. The Keeper with the whip had a chilling smile on his face, a feral snarl ripping from his chest with each lash that he delivered against the boy's back.

Beside Aera, Phantom froze in shock. There was a woman at

the front of the crowd, deep wrinkles lining her worn cheeks. Her face was contorted with grief and tears ran down her face. Aera assumed it was the boy's mother. "Please stop," she pleaded quietly, hands clasped in front of her as if she itched to help her son. The Keeper ignored her. After a few more lashes, the Keeper wiped his bloody face on his sleeve, his mouth tipping up into a twisted grin. He set down the bronze whip and held his hands out to touch the boys back. At the Keeper's cool touch, the boy cringed and moved his hands closer to the iron pole.

"I hope you have learned today," the Keeper said lowly, gently. "You must call me Keeper Logan; nothing else. If you disobey me like you did, I'll be forced to punish you." He leaned closer to the boy. "Do it again, and I'll use the gold whip next time." He chuckled darkly. He then spat at the boy's feet and walked away with his brown whip coiled around his arm like a snake.

Phantom broke from his trance and gave Aera another light push. "We have to keep walking." As he disappeared into the foggy depths of the camp, the older woman ran up to the boy, sobbing. She pulled a sharp knife from her pocket, cutting the spiked iron from around his wrists and freeing him from the stake. The boy touched his bleeding hands and gave his mother a reassuring smile.

"I'm okay, mother. You must return to the factory before you are whipped as well." He gently guided his sobbing mother in the direction a large building with stacks of smoke rising from giant metal cylinders.

Phantom looked about as traumatized as Aera felt. She glanced back at the raven-haired boy, and he looked back at her. His eyes were red. Aera gasped and turned away, walking even quicker than before. It wasn't long until they reached a large compound, much larger and cleaner than anything else she'd seen in the camp. When they walked in, the two felt like they'd stepped into a completely different place. It was a gourmet kitchen; the demons were clean in white aprons and hats, shouting and cooking. Some demons were in tight blue jumpers, mopping the floor and washing dishes. Aera almost smiled, but then she caught Phantom's angry stare.

"They treat the kitchen staff this well...but only because they are preparing the humans' food. They can't afford to cook in dirty, unsanitary conditions." He explained, jaw tight.

With this knowledge, the kitchen appeared just as horrible as everything else. She looked towards a boy with shaggy brown hair and light silver eyes. When the name came to her, she nearly burst with joy. "Luke?"

The boy looked up, his eyes bright. "Aera? What are you doing here?"

She opened her mouth to respond, but suddenly, a roaring sound came from outside.

Phantom ran outside, and Aera was close on his heels.

In the middle of the camp, there was a boy with silver wings. He passed a bright smile at the Phantom, and said, "I'm here to save you, little brother." He looked at Aera, and his eyes flickered in recognition.

"I'm here to save you too Opposite Air." He smiled.

To be continued...

9 780974 226989

Printed by Libri Plureos GmbH in Hamburg,
Germany